James Mayhew
presents

Ella Bella
BALLERINA
~ and ~
Cinderella

For my Finnish pen-friend's daughter
~ Eveliina ~

First edition for the United States, its territories and dependencies, and Canada
published in 2009 by Barron's Educational Series, Inc.

Text and illustrations © James Mayhew 2009

First published in 2009 by Orchard Books
338 Euston Road
London, NW1 3BH

All inquiries should be addressed to:
Barron's Educational Series, Inc.
250 Wireless Blvd.
Hauppauge, NY 11788
www.barronseduc.com

ISBN-13: 978-0-7641-6268-8
ISBN-10: 0-7641-6268-3

Library of Congress Catalog No.: 2009921953

Date of Manufacture: March 2013
Manufactured by: South China Printing Co., Dongguan, China

Printed in China
9 8 7 6 5 4

James Mayhew
presents

Ella Bella
BALLERINA
and
Cinderella

BARRON'S

Ella Bella ran up the steps of the old theater.
She couldn't wait for Madame Rosa's ballet class
to begin.

Ella Bella quickly got ready for the lesson,
but when she looked in her bag,
She could only find one ballet shoe . . .

"Don't worry, darling," said Madame Rosa.
"I have lots of spares."
She opened up a trunk filled with beautiful
shoes and found a pair for Ella Bella.

"You remind me of Cinderella," said Madame Rosa. "She also lost a shoe! Let us dance to the *Cinderella* ballet music."

Madame Rosa opened the special musical box — a beautiful tune began to play and the little ballerina inside spun around. The children began to dance as well.

"Can you tell us about Cinderella?" asked Ella Bella.

"Well, she dreamed of going to the Royal Ball at the palace, but her wicked stepsisters made her stay behind to do all the housework!" said Madame Rosa.

"Poor Cinderella!" sighed the class.

The children danced and
danced until all too soon
the music stopped and
the lesson was over.

"Time to get changed,
everyone," said Madame Rosa.
"Come along, Ella Bella."

But Ella Bella wasn't really
listening. She was thinking
about Cinderella . . .

Alone on the stage, Ella Bella opened the lid
of Madame Rosa's box.

The *Cinderella* music played, and as Ella Bella
began to dance it grew louder and louder . . .

Suddenly, dancing fairies in different
colors surrounded Ella Bella!
The most beautiful of them bowed down.
"I am Cinderella's fairy godmother,"
she said. "And these are the Fairies
of the Four Seasons."

"Poor Cinderella!"
said Spring.

"Everyone has gone to
the Royal Ball, except
her!" said Summer.

"She has no carriage or
gown . . ." said Autumn.

" . . . and no shoes,"
sighed Winter.

Ella Bella opened the trunk and took out a pair of
silver shoes. "Will these do for Cinderella?" she asked.
"Let's see!" said the fairy godmother.

She waved her wand, and with a twinkling
of magic they were in the kitchen of
a grand house. Cinderella
sat weeping by the fire.

"Come now," said her fairy godmother.
"You shall go to the Ball."
"But I have nothing to wear!" sniffed Cinderella.

The Fairies of the Four Seasons waved
their wands . . . and Cinderella found
she was wearing a magnificent gown.

Then Ella Bella
gave Cinderella
the silver shoes.
"Oh, thank you!"
said Cinderella.
"They fit perfectly!"

"Now, go with her, Ella Bella," said the
fairy godmother. "But you must be
home by midnight — not even fairy
magic can last forever!"
And with a wave of her wand,
a golden carriage appeared.

The enchanted carriage swept them
off to the palace, while above
them the stars danced in the sky.

Inside, the Royal Ball had started.
Everyone looked splendid, but
Cinderella was the loveliest by far.

The prince stepped forward.
"Please may I have this dance?"
he asked Cinderella.

The prince and Cinderella danced all evening.
"It's not fair!" said an angry girl.
"Why doesn't he dance with us?" said another.
Ella Bella thought they must be Cinderella's
stepsisters. They hadn't recognized Cinderella
in her beautiful gown.

Just then, the clock began to chime . . . it was
MIDNIGHT! Ella Bella tugged Cinderella's dress.
"We must go!" she cried.

They ran down the steps of the palace
and as the last chime rang out, Cinderella's
beautiful gown changed back into old rags.

"Oh, no!" gasped Cinderella. "The prince must not see me like this!"

As Cinderella hurried off, Ella Bella saw she had left one of Madame Rosa's silver shoes behind!

Ella Bella ran back up the steps . . . and there
stood the prince, holding the silver shoe.
"I will search the world to find the girl who
lost this shoe!" he said.

"I know where she lives!" said Ella Bella.
"Then please take me there!" said the prince.

They passed through forests and over mountains
until at last they came to Cinderella's house.

"I shall marry the girl whose foot fits this shoe!" said the prince.
The stepsisters rushed to try it on . . . but their feet were too big!

All of a sudden, the matching shoe fell from Cinderella's apron pocket.
The prince wondered . . . could this be the beautiful girl he had danced with?

Cinderella put on the shoes.
They fit perfectly!
All the fairies flew down and exclaimed,
"Well done, Ella Bella! You helped Cinderella
find a happy ending!"

The prince and Cinderella danced for joy,
and the beautiful music filled the air,
growing louder and louder . . .

And then, Ella Bella was all alone on the empty
stage once more, and the musical box was silent.
In her hands were the silver shoes. She slowly
returned them to the trunk, with the pair she
had borrowed for herself.

"Good girl!" said Madame Rosa, bustling
onto the stage. "Now, hurry along, or you'll
be late for your dinner!"
"Thank you," said Ella Bella. "I loved
dancing to the *Cinderella* ballet music."

"Cinder . . . *ella* . . ." smiled Madame Rosa.
"You even share her name, but try to remember
both your shoes next time!"
"I'll try," laughed Ella Bella. "Goodbye!"
"Goodbye, darling!" said Madame Rosa, as Ella
Bella and her mother skipped down the street.

Sergei Prokofiev's ballet *Cinderella* is based on the famous version of the story by Charles Perrault. This tale includes a glass slipper, a pumpkin that becomes a carriage and, of course, a fairy godmother, but Prokofiev's ballet is a little different . . . There are no glass slippers — perhaps Prokofiev thought they would be impossible to dance in — instead, Cinderella's slippers are special dancing shoes! Also, although most modern performances include the famous pumpkin carriage, it is not in Prokofiev's original ballet, which has Cinderella whisked off to the ball by a beautiful ballet of twinkling stars! See if you can spot a pumpkin *and* the dancing stars in this book . . . And lastly, instead of just a fairy godmother, the ballet features the Fairies of the Four Seasons.

Prokofiev composed several ballets, including *Romeo and Juliet* and *The Stone Flower*. But his most famous piece for children isn't a ballet at all — it is for an orchestra and a storyteller, and it's called *Peter and the Wolf*.

Although other composers had used the famous Cinderella story, Prokofiev's ballet is the most well known, perhaps because of the stirring and magical music, which helps us imagine all those wonderful characters.